A Glimpse from Christmas Past

By: D. C. Donahue

Illustrated by
Stephen Adams

Rich & Maureen,
Enjoy sharing your
traditions with your
family!
Love,
Joe & Karen

AuthorHouse™
1663 Liberty Drive
Bloomington, IN 47403
www.authorhouse.com
Phone: 1-800-839-8640

Published by AuthorHouse 04/10/2013

ISBN: 978-1-4817-4028-9 (sc)
978-1-4817-4027-2 (e)

Library of Congress Control Number: 2013906594

Any people depicted in stock imagery provided by Thinkstock are models,
and such images are being used for illustrative purposes only.
Certain stock imagery © Thinkstock.

This book is printed on acid-free paper.

Because of the dynamic nature of the Internet, any web addresses or links contained in this book may have changed
since publication and may no longer be valid. The views expressed in this work are solely those of the author and do not
necessarily reflect the views of the publisher, and the publisher hereby disclaims any responsibility for them.

authorHOUSE®

Edited By: Nancy Donahue

Illustrated By: (Author House Publishing)

Dedication:

To my wife Nancy, our children and grandchildren: Who without their love, support and inspiration this book would not have been possible.

To Our Parents, Families and Friends both living and deceased: For the parts they played in making us who we are today.

6

It was Christmas Eve, when snow started lightly falling down. There I was gifts in hand, as I hustled through the town. The stores were all opened, as their lights twinkled with life. Streets were bustling with shoppers, with last minute gifts in flight. Salvation Army bell ringers were stationed at many corners and stores. They'd offer 'Seasons Greetings', in soliciting for the needy, the poor. Main Street was strung with garland and wreaths that ran from pole to pole…to City Hall down Broad Street where the Mummers soon would stroll. There, William Penn stood with a grin; smiling down on the carolers below. Oh, what a beautiful town this is when covered in a blanket of snow.

Now finished with shopping I pulled on my gloves stepping out into the night. I turned a collar to the cold, wrapping my scarf around tight. The pavements now newly coated were slowing everything down. The streets were covered as buses and cars slushed their way through town. Thinking of nights like tonight and how much colder downtown always seemed…maybe it's due to the big buildings being surrounded by rivers and streams? Carefully I walked, rounding a corner, so not to slip or fall. When glancing into a shop window I was taken by surprise and awe.

One last child, list in hand, stood anxiously beaming with delight…waiting to see Santa, in full regalia, on this magical wondrous night. Gently he lifted the child to his lap with a roar of a laugh and a smile. I watched him whisper in their ear, listening intently all the while. They told him of the gifts they wanted as he assured them he would try. Saying, 'only if you promise to be good all year', as he waited their reply.

He said, "the elves keep me in the know of the children who are naughty or nice. So, be sure to listen to your parents and teachers; heeding their advice". He added, "don't forget to leave some goodies on a table by the door…as this business of delivering toys and gifts is certainly no easy chore". Then as he lifted the child down, I was staring at myself through the glass. Suddenly remembering the faces and places at a Glimpse from a Christmas Past.

10

I thought of a time, when shopping with my parents, who now both are gone.   It was always Sister Nancy, Larry and me who always seemed to be tagging along.   First stop was Gimbel's to see Santa, while our parents warned that we'd better be good.   Then it was onto the H&H Automat, for some milkshakes and a bite of food.   Next stop was Lit Brother's, to Old London Town, and their "Dickens' Village" display.   You could walk the cobblestone streets of Marley and Scrooge; where the Cratchett children all played.   You can look on with Scrooge, to a corner by the fireplace, where there stands a crutch by a vacant stool.   But not after the ghosts of Christmas have all visited; showing Ebenezer he was just an old fool.   We always ended at Wanamaker's, timing it, to see the Christmas fountain and light show.   We'd try to get there early to sit atop the Eagle or get a good spot on the floor.

It was then I looked up from the child in the window and as Santa's eyes met mine; that he smiled at me scratching his head sending me to a certain place and time. It was a memory from my childhood in a moment we both had shared. It suddenly came rushing back to me and I knew he too was aware. It was another cold snowy Christmas Eve so much like that of tonight. I was maybe five going on six, no wait, six going on seven; surely that had to be right. I remembered so clearly that lost memory from way back in sixty-three. I had decided to hide to find, to see what I could see. I was finally going to rest aside the myths of my older siblings and friends. That Santa wasn't just a regular guy but someone I also knew as a friend!

I remembered placing a plate of carrots and cookies on a table beside a tall glass of milk. I was hunkered behind a tall chair by the fireplace, wrapped in a blanket of silk. I had some time to wonder of things that I never gave much thought to before. Did Santa really eat all those cookies left by the children of the world by their doors? Well at least that explained why Santa became a ripe, plump and jolly old elf. But I quickly let this weighty thought escape me laughing quietly to myself. I switched my thoughts to reindeer eating carrots; wouldn't they prefer some good hay or straw? But I knew such thoughts wouldn't be good, if I was to get a new bike at all. Yawning, I let my mind wonder to the grand entrance he was surely to make. Maybe he'd enter the house through a doorway, or down the chimney for tradition's sake? Perhaps he'd come in the front door using some elf dust or magic keys; or just pop in through a latched window, ever so nonchalantly.

I just started drifting off when I heard jingle bells not so far away. They seemed to come from across the road or just down the way. So I peeked out the window, rubbing my eyes, to the glistening street below. The trees and cars were covered in white as nothing moved in the street light's warm glow. It was then I got a glimpse of him, as the reindeer danced in the air. He made driving the sleigh look simple, as he handled the reins with care. They darted quickly from a neighbor's rooftop to settle on our home. The sled landed softly in a whoosh, as I tensed with excitement that shown. As the reindeer were settling from their prancing and pawing, on the eaves up above; Santa swiftly climbed down swiping the snow from the chimney, using his sturdy gloves.

He came bounding down with a quiet thud, taking long looks around, with a smile. He placed his sack on the floor, wiped his brow then decided to sit for a while. He stepped softly to the chair I was hidden behind just as natural as can be. He called me by name to my astonishment saying, "come and visit with me". He stood looking me over through glasses that sat precariously on the end of his nose. As he rocked back and forth, hands clasped behind him swaying from heel to toe. He said, "I knew you were there all along, as nothing escapes me you see! If I was fooled, by every child hiding to catch me, what kind of elf would I be"!

I asked if he'd like the cookies and milk or prefer something warm instead. He answered, 'that would be really nice' as he pushed his cap back scratching his head. I asked if he'd prefer hot cocoa or tea, to take the chill from his bones. He said, "Either one sounds good to me" as I ran to put the water on. He followed me into the kitchen taking a seat by the stove. He asked if I had any questions; I said 'perhaps a few I suppose'.

How do the elves help make it possible to deliver all the gifts, in one single night? What magic was used in giving the reindeer the miracle of flight? He said "whoa slow down I'm hungry, could you fetch the cookies from the other room…if I'm to get through your inquisition, before continuing my long journey home". He answered my many questions as we chatted between sips of tea. Then asked me to promise to keep these secrets while politely reaching for another cookie. He placed the empty cup on his saucer as he brushed the last of the crumbs from his beard. He said, tapping his head," I must not forget the carrots for my trusty reindeer".

Thanking each other as we stood he asked if I was pleased with our visit tonight?   "You bet "! I replied walking to the other room where I was struck by an amazing sight. The stockings were full; the tree now decorated, surrounded with gifts neatly stacked on the floor.   There was something for everyone with my new bike tucked away, in a corner by the door.   Oh! It was black and white with a red pin stripe running down the length of the frame. There were gifts for the whole family mixed amongst packages, toys and games.   I stood there stunned, mouth wide open as I turned to thank him with a smile. How could this be, as we sat sipping tea eating cookies and chatting the whole while??

I spun around to thank him again as he flung his sack on his back. He said 'remember me always in the spirit of the One who allows me each year to come back. He blessed me to mark this, His holy day, on the calendars of the world to be looked upon... as the light from the star that showed the way to where Mary and Joseph smiled down on their Son. I bring gifts to the children in the same manner of the three kings who paid homage from distant lands... like the angels who heralded the news of Jesus's birth to every woman, child and man.

He then said "I think it's time you get to bed as I really must be on my way". Then turned in a flash with a nod and a smile as up the chimney he flew to his sleigh. I heard him call to excited prancing and pawing as he urged his trusty steeds to flight. I ran to the window as he flew across the moonlit sky saying 'Merry Christmas to all a Goodnight!!

Then just as fast as my dream had begun I was back staring at him once again through the glass. I was the same older man, with gifts still in hand, as he smiled remembering our past. He gave me a knowing wink tapping his head as the shopkeeper locked the door. He smiled and waved as I was turning away he wished me Merry Christmas once more. It was just after seven, going on eight, as I boarded my train in the subways below. I took the R3 to Gladstone Manor, to my waiting car covered in snow.

I finally came to our street, was entering the house, when the children sent up the alarm. They ushered me in and as I kicked off my boots my wife glided into my arms. She kissed me as she pointed up for me to see some mistletoe hung above the door. The younger children ran away ewwing and screaming hoping there wouldn't be any more. We gave chase as they ran giggling and laughing into the other room. They were full of delight at the snow outside and that Santa would be visiting soon. I looked up just as our older son was putting the angel on top of the tree. As he stepped down from the ladder saying "Merry Christmas Dad", I thought of how this tradition had passed from me.

We hope you enjoyed this story and find it worthy of a place on your shelf; where it can be quickly grabbed each year at Christmas time to be read until you pass it on to be enjoyed for years to come by your loved ones.

"May you and yours always be able to share the warmth of the holiday season throughout the years"

In word's best said by my sister, Mary -   (G.A.K.Y.S.)

THE END

Reader Notes

CPSIA information can be obtained
at www.ICGtesting.com
Printed in the USA
BVIC01n0927300913
3323/0BV00002B